Angraiyaan

"Angraiyaan"

ISBN No: " 978-93-90416-99-8"
1st Edition
Language – English and Hindi

Flairs and Glairs
Publication House
Regd. Under MSME Act.

Disclaimer

This is a work of fiction and solely represent the thoughts of the corresponding authors of the articles. Our editors have tried their best to edit the content of all the authors and check the plagiarism.

All the write-ups in this book are unique and are only published in this book.

In case any plagiarism or error is found, only the author is responsible alone, and not the publisher or the Compilers.

Cover Designing
Shubham Shah

Acknowledgement

Dear Almighty, thank you for blessing me with the power and zeal to be able to complete this Anthology. Also, Thank You dear parents, for trusting in me, and letting me work whenever I wanted. My family is the one who supported me for what I am today.
When it comes to this Anthology, I would like to start with Thanking the Co-authors, without your help and support, I would have never been able to complete it.

Thank You all of you, for being there. Much Love to all of You. I am glad to see you all standing by me.

Co Authors

1. Shubham Shah (Founder Flairs and Glairs)
2. Ishani Agarwal (Co Founder Flairs and Glairs)
3. Shivangi Jaiswal (Compiler)
4. Saheb Ghosh
5. Jayati Thakar
6. Heena Shaikh Mulla
7. Adarsh Kumar Priyadarshi
8. Sanjida Khan
9. Deepjyoti Chowdhury
10. Shaily Tyagi
11. Meenakshi Sharma
12. Maitreyee
13. Abhilash Rout
14. Parwana Bibi
15. Sachin Banoudhiya
16. Astha Yadav
17. Prachi Gupta
18. Ayesha Rajpal
19. Shobha Rajpal
20. Shajeela Shamreen
21. Smriti Kumari
22. Sahina Ghugha
23. Siya Golani
24. Khushbu Rathore
25. Muskan Sachdeva

26.Lokesh Upadhyay.
27.Ujjwal Shree
28.Prakash Sharma
29.Ashwini Kumar Singh
30.Neha. M
31.Saurabh Rajput
32.Vedika Agarwal
33.Shubham Kumar
34.Abhishek Rawat
35.Debanjana Ghatak
36.Pratham Mittal
37.Pragya Verma
38.Siya Golani
39.Jainab Natchiya. Y
40.Sanoj Kumar
41.Kalamkaar
42.Shivam Sinha
43.Yamini Sona Vaishnavi
44.Sunil Kimidi
45.Pragyan Panda
46.Hema Kirthiga J
47.Vikash Kumar Bhakat
48.Ekta Pankaj Bathija
49.Swayamdeepta Das
50.Shivani Taneja
51.Chirag L Sagar
52.Ajay Poddar 'Anmol
53.Dr Rakesh R Mund

Shubham Shah

(Founder- Flairs and Glairs)

Shubham Shah, entrepreneur at "Flairs & Glairs" a brand with dynamics in events organizing and cultural educational pan INDIA, He is a 26yr. old guy who recently has entered, the digital platform of imprinting emotions. He has initiated with his own open mic platform to help budding poets and aspiring writers under his brand named as "Teekhe Zasbaaat"
He is a commerce graduate from Bhagalpur City of Bihar.
He says Writing has impersonated him since childhood and he has now been writing for over a decade!
Cooking, on the other hand, is his passion! He also mentions, trying out new things just tickles him!

When asked sir, Why SPICY EMOTIONS?
He smiled and added, “agar jasbaat teekhe na ho toh wo jasbaat kaha” Spices are all that blends! So do his words!
As a chef, he presents to you his dish! Hot and freshly served! Taste it! Feel it! Enjoy it! You can also find his writing in the Solo book “Teekhe Zasbaaat” and 70+ anthologies. With his passion to explore opportunities across Platforms he is working with keen devotion and We wish him all the very best for his future ventures
Share your reviews on his

INSTAGRAM

@spicy_emotions
@shubham4shah

Or via email on

shubham2shah@gmail.com

To stay tuned to his work and opportunities follow his business Handles

INSTAGRAM FACEBOOK YOUTUBE

@flairsandglairs
@teekhezasbaaat

WEBSITE:

https://flairsandglairs.in/
https://flairsandglairs.com/

Ishani Agarwal

(Co Founder- Flairs and Glairs)

Ishani Agarwal
Born and brought up in Kolkata, she has done her schooling and college from here itself. She is doing her post-graduation at the moment. Ishani loves talking to people around, and is excited for this new beginning of hers! Been a Compiler for 35+ Anthologies, and in the process for more, also, co-authored in 100+ Anthologies, Ishani is very Happy with how her life is turning out now!
Insta handle: Ishani_agarwal_quotes

Shivangi Jaiswal

(Compiler)

Shivangi Jaiswal is a Content Writer from Kolkata. Project Head & Coordinator at “Flairs & Glairs” brand with dynamics in events organizing and cultural educational pan INDIA. Organiser at "The Glittering Fables" Writing Community. She is a B.Com Honours graduate. Certified in Stocks & Short Selling as well as Certified in Digital Marketing Been a keen student, she has recently been Certified for learning Spanish Language..She loves to bring smiles and happiness to many faces, so she is into social service. Shivangi has also done her Diploma in painting, drawing and all kinds of clay making, craft works. Traveler, Teacher, Meditator, Dancer, Singer, Instrument Player. She loves to play guitar and harmonium. Been a public speaker she has taken part in many events and nailed it. Also been a great Advisor to many. Sports freak of Swimming and Badminton with a passion so strong. Since, past one year she has started her writing journey. She writes so that many people can connect with their stories and get positive hopes. She thinks " Every story is unique so embrace yourself to the best".She is a writer by day and a reader by night. Been a Complier of 20+ Anthologies, and in process for more, also Co- authored 60+ anthologies. Shivangi is an old soul with young eyes, a vintage heart, and a beautiful mind."

You can follow her work:
Instagram
@the_knockingvibe
@house_of_compilations

Morning Bliss

Morning Bliss is life,
The sun heading over so elegant and bright.
The breeze touching my cheeks,
Makes me alive.

I kiss the flowers, and smell divine.
And shake the dew that fallen in the night.
So bright is the sky, I stare with my magical eyes.
The Lily's blossom pure as white.

The birds chirping their song with divine.
I rise with the morning so beautiful,
wanting to hug it all day.
The rosy light falling on my skin.
The sun kissing me with a beautiful light.

My morning, my happy thing.
Dwell all over me.
Because light is here vanishing all the darkness.
Gliding the heaven, the sun appears.

For everyone, that is softly taken.
How sweet it is?
To wait for the sweet morn.
With a kiss of dew.

Fresh Mornings.

Oh! My Fresh mornings.
The rosy morning's that glow over me.
As I wake up with a smile and sun kissed face.
When mists go by, I hear the heavenly song of the birds singing.

Morning's is sweeter, as I taste the Sunkissed hue.
Looking at the day so new.
That makes me smile all day.
Morning is so beautiful, as it is a perfect start of the day.

Love and Hope finds a new way.
You can feel up at cloud nine.
Love of mine, you share with yourself.
Right through heart and soul that makes you everlasting divine.
The power of vibe you feel all day, with elegance and bright.

The morning's whisper magical words.
That enlightenment that glow and vanishes the sadness away.
Oh! My darling morning.
Lying warm near me.
Now and forever.
Better and better.
A bright Good Morning,
to the freshest cool spark.

Saheb Ghosh

Saheb Ghosh, a poet who loves nature very much. He believes in simplicity and he also indisputably believe that God is the reason of all reasons. He writes poem, essay and short story both in English and Bengali.

Tricky Pillow

Every morning, I have to be scolded;
My mother says, you will never be amended.
I, like a brassy, listen her and forget,
But sometimes it makes my rank derogate.

I sleep and sleep, till the morning passes
My sleep can not be broken by shouting masses.
My father extremely tries to wake me up,
But I am sticked with the bed never get up.

Whenever, I try to get up early morning;
My pillow says me, where am I going.
For it, I think, I should sleep more awhile;
After waking up, I presume it's all the pillow's guile.

Jayati Thakar

A girl Pursued Masters in Arts with major English Literature. She lives in Bhavnagar, a city in Gujarat. She has been appeared in three different national and international literary conferences and represented her research work in varies of different literary criteria of Criticism, Feminism and Cultural Studies. She loves to learn various of foreign languages and study their culture through watching their dramas and series in their own languages. She with her jovial way of lifestyle, used to entertain her surroundings. Deeply in love to roam around the glob; yet not started her journey. She loves to cook and to dance. She has more powerful sides than the other as emotional and caring for her dear ones. She is ambitious. And she is skilled at multiple duties at her great interests like event handling, teaching and counseling. Withal she is good at interacting to the people about their problems at her personal interest to study human psychology carved deep within. Not so good reader at once she is, but with a little effort she tries to give wings to her words and till now has participated in more than ten anthologies and yet pursuing for more.

(1)

Morning spreads through my home like,
It's eager to enter in my room since dawn, and as if it has been waiting for curtains be offed, so it can get in and greet me "morning" further it burst like a dazzling flash on my face, withal this, it just boost me up to initiate a new fine day. (Morning Vibes)

Light Me Up Like

A first ray of sun which tears between mountains and shades between branches every day. Which symbolise the rise of dawn as a green hope for a another new day, which used to inspire you in the past and yet has not given up on you. Which is there to push you head forward, so you live on gracefully along with your miseries turning into melodies.

I Bloom Every Morning,

I Bloom Every Morning
With the recalling the name of my Lord thanking Him to include one more fine day in my life,
one cup of chaay is the perfect start to seize the day fresh,
Listening to the singings of roaming birds around and the favourite tracks while swinging early in the morning is like a melody to ears and remedy to heart and the soul,
"finally with picking up a pen and ink my heart out on paper"
- that's how I initiates my day sweet and sound.

Heena Shaikh Mulla

Heena Shaikh Mulla is from Pune,currently residing in Karnataka.She's from an ICSE background,graduated from Pune University(MSC Computer Science). She's the author of 'Technical Desserts' and also holds a Vajra record for the same.

Besides being a college topper,She likes drawing henna, teaching and fantasizes about Polar Bears.

She's a charming personality who expresses her thoughts in the form of Poetry and Shayri and currently she's compiling books as well.

Naya Savera

Har badte kadam k saath,
Manzil dikhti hai aur sunheri.

Har toofan k guzarne k baad,
Milti hai rahat pyaari.

Har ek paani k boond k saath,
Bujti hai pyaar gehari.

Har andheri raat k baad,
Aata hai ek naya savera.

Aankhe khol kar toh dekh,
Zindagi Jeene ki umaga hai angraiyo se bhi pare.

Kosish jaari rakho,
Kamiyabi mil hi jayegi kisi mod par.

Adarsh Kumar Priyadarshi

Adarsh Kumar Priyadarshi is a school going boy form a small town called Hajipur, Bihar. His father servers the nation in Indian Army. And his mother is a housemarker. He is co-author of 40+ anthology . As he is proud to be the son of a loyal army man so he too wants to do something great for his mother-land. As he has a great zeal in medical field so he is currently even struggling with his journey to reach his destination, his goal i.e. to be a renowned doctor. He always thanks his parents, teachers, friend and God for what he is now.

His debut, book will be launched soon.

Five More Minutes

Wake up, Wake up......
The sun is on your head
Get up from your bed
You are too lazy
Everyone will hate.

Mom just five minutes
I slept late.
This is the excuse I made.
But this is not going help.
You have to get up
As they thought it is right.

Sanjida Khan

Sanjida is a student at Vidhaan Public School. She likes to write and sketch.

Bachpan Ki Vo Angraiyaan

Yaad hai bachpan ka vo morning alarm...
Or yaad hai vo alarm sunkr angraiya lena..
Subha ki vo angraiya lena or maa se kehna..
Bs aankhein band hain uth to gya hu...
Sardiyo me rajayi me ghuse rhte subha uthne ka mann na krta..
Bs sochte ke kaash aaj sunday hota...
Or bistar me angraiya lete..
Yaad hai bss 5 min or fir pakka uth jaunga kehkr school ke liye late ho jaana..
Kaash vo din firse laut paate..
Or firse hum bistar pr angraiya le paate..

Deepjyoti Chowdhury

Deepjyoti Chowdhury embraces reading and writing as her escape from the real world as well as a window to it. She is a strong believer of Christ and Karma. Written in 100+ anthologies, she is the author of "Heartfelt musings" and "The staircase to freedom". Her main aim is to heal people and make them smile through her art of writing. You can follow her on Instagram at dj_writes_to_heal

Morning Delight

During the mornings when we hesitate to leave the bed,
And the comfort of the quilt pulls back our head.
The sweet dreams that we assume is always true,
For an extra five minute of sleep we often argue.
Blissful is the chirping of bird and the cuckoo.
Into the dreamland we get lost and it continues.
Until the harsh alarm wakes us up from the sleep,
Pulling us out of the unconsciousness that's deep.
Unwillingly we have to pull up ourselves,
After the rest of sleep, we find a new strength.
A fresh new day hence we all start,
And from the comfort of the bed we finally depart.

Shaily Tyagi

She is a born writer, a compiler and a dreamer who seems to win hearts by her deeds. Here she is with her poem. Hope all will like it.

सुबह की वह पहली हंसी

तुम सुबह कि वह पहली हंसी हो,
जैसे बादलों से निकलकर खूबसूरत धूप खिली हो,
तुम सुबह का वह पहला सपना हो,
अनजान रास्तों पर जैसे कोई अपना हो,
जिंदगी एक है पर सपने हजार हैं,
बस तुमसे मिलने को यह मन बेकरार है,
ना फिकर किसी की भी,
बस तुम्हारा ही खुमार है,
तुम नहीं तो कुछ नहीं,
तुम हो तो जिंदगी में बहार है।
ख्वाहिश है दिल की हर ख्वाहिश में तुम रहो,
आंखें ना खोलो मैं,
जिस सपने में तुम रहो।

Meenakshi Sharma

Meenakshi Sharma, a creative writer and poetess is always ready to do something new and believes that she will surely get her goal one day.

"एक बार जब.... "

एक दिन अपने काम से
हम पहुंचे देहरादून
देर हो गई रात में
रुक गए लेकर रूम
कमरा था वह छोटा सा
पड़ी थी एक चार पाई
जैसे तैसे रात कटेगी
ले लेकर अंगडाई
थके हुए थे दिन भर से
अब रात में भी ना सुकून
एक तो चारपाई में कांटे खटमल
ऊपर से मच्छर चूसे खून
पूरी रात करवटें बदलते तब आंखें भर आई
सवेरे थोड़ी हवा चली नींद हमें तब आइ
सुबह सवेरे हमको तो पकड़नी थी ट्रेन
बैठे बैठे हुआ सवेरा तब आई हमें चैन
सोचा था दो पल की एक झपकी सी ले लूं
आंखें अपनी खुले समय से अलार्म सेट कर लूं अलार्म समय से लगा बजने

पर अब आंख नहीं खुल पाई

अलार्म को तो बंद करके सो गए मुन्ना भाई

सोते-सोते झट से जागे लगा नींद पर ब्रेक

घड़ी में झट से टाइम देखा

हाय हो गए हम तो लेट

Maitreyee

She is Maitreyee. Don't go by her age since she can bemuse you with her words. She is bubbly, scintilating and ambitious. She holds expertise in story telling, micro tales and also knows how to weave words into beautiful poetries. She is a foodie and also loves cooking.

The Struggle Is Real...! ~

'Sleep' and 'I' have been in a constant relationship from the very moment I unveiled that there is nothing that can compare to the loyalty and commitment that sleep can provide! Yes, food is ans exception though but never mind.

While I've seen people breaking up, falling apart, blaming each other and then ultimately blaming the ' sleepless nights ' for all their miseries. How?? and why??. How does sleep has anything to do with your heartbreaks and relationships. The fact is these people are themselves never loyal enough to anybody or anything.

Well about me, I would say that the Struggle is Real. Every morning when the whole world wakes up, gets ready to follow their tedious routine that too with full exuberance, I am there lying on my bed, beside my fluffy cute teddy and wonder what is so exciting in life that people give up their sleep, their comfort for things that are unsure and mysterious? And then here, I get my answer.

Though sleep is bae, but work is worship. There is definitely something nee and mysterious in every coming day, nee challenges, hopes, excitement, surprises. But for all this we need to get out of our comfort zones, compromise a little on our sleep.

Yes, indeed The Struggle is Real. but it is Worth every moment...!

Abhilash Rout

Abhilash Rout is from Cuttack, Odisha.

He has completed his graduation in B.Com with Accounts Honours.He is preparing for competitive exams too. He has been working for the welfare of working out for the weaker sections of the society.

Writing has been a part of expressing his feelings & his thoughts into words.He is working in Odia film industry as an actor, story writer and assistant director.His Instagram handle is @coolcapt_abhilash.

He has taken part in more than 115 anthologies which includes international anthologies too.

Resistance of Getting Up in The Morning

We go through different phases in life,
where we fail to do anything.
Sometimes, the difficult situations in our
life is when we come across a situation
that we have promised ourselves that
we will get up early in the morning and
start doing something good.
But the saddest reality is that we cannot
keep our own words because many a
times we fail miserably in the aspects in
which we have promised ourselves.
The most difficult task we really face is that
sometimes we are not able to wake up in
the morning and it really creates a mess
when we have promised someone about
helping them by waking up in the morning.

Reality of Life

We come across such a situations
in our life,
where we become lazy and we really
end up getting into problems.
Nowadays, everyone have become
little bit lazy as the passage of time
and the development of technology.
As the time passes by people have
actually changes their health policies,
in the ancient days people used to get
up very early and nowadays it's just
the opposite.
Before people used to follow the rules
of sleeping early and getting up early.
With the advancement of technologies
people are now sleeping very very late
in the morning.
So we should avoid doing that.

Parwana Bibi

Parwana Bibi a little moody and shy girl . She want to see people happy and she is so cute . She is very talented and never give up any situation. Let's see what she write for us.

।।अंगड़ाई ।।

।। आज अंगड़ाई मेरी मुझसे जुदा होने को नाराज़ है
जब जब उठती हूँ तो फिर यह अंगड़ाई नीन्द की आग़ोश में डुबो देती है ।।

।। आज मौसम बहुत ही राहत वाला लगता है
और नीन्द से उठने की चाहत यह अंगड़ाई पूरी नहीं होने देती है ।।

Subha Ki Angdai

Meri subha ki angdai tumhare chehero ko dekh kar aur bhi hasin jo jate hain ,
Jab tum pass nahi hote ho to subha ki angdaiyan tumhe dhundte hain .....
Angdaiyan meri mujh se yeh keheti hai ki tumhe dekhe bina bistar se nah uthhein ,
Aur fir sara din beet jata hai tumhari yaadon ke panho mein .....

Sachin Banoudhiya

He is a student of Bsc
A Struggling Writter now Started Getting so many platforms
He Loves to do Audio Poetries & video Editing .
He's a Publish Co - author in so many Anthologies

Resistance Of Getting Up In The Morning

The Reason of that Resistance is that late night scrolling On Insta , YouTube , Facebook . We Stucked On The Screen . We have to understand That Netflix won't give us a better sleep

Feel the night vibes ,that Peace , that nature Sound , Like they are saying Blacked Out your mind & hear the Silence & Get a Best Sleep

Rising With The Sun Feels You The Bestest Coolest Sweetest Reaction of Sun .
The Sleep Is The Better Option Rather then that Late night chatting .
When You get up You've to forgot that you've a Cell phone
If You start your day with scrolling
No one can stop you From That

Resistance of Getting Up in The Morning

Astha Yadav

Astha Yadav is from Uttar Pradesh. She's an amateur writer who loves to spill her emotions on the pages of her diary. Astha has participated in more than fifty books as a co-author including record holder books. She has compiled eight books till date. She's a vajra world records holder herself. Her only dream is to make her parents proud and happy.

Insta id- red_rose431

Early Risers

Sleeping at 3 a.m. and rising at 12 p.m. has become a new trend. But it has some really dangerous effects on the mental and physical ability of this generation. Some of them are not aware of the benefits of early rising and some are really careless to spend their time on phones till late at night, rather than giving rest to their body.

Early rising is nice for human, because it is claimed that "early to bed early to rise, makes a person healthy, affluent and wise." By rising early we get tendency to remain active whole day.

The scientifically well-tried benefit of this habit, is "exercise in morning". Early morning is the best part of the day. Birds begin to chirp, flower open up to the rays of sun, the breeze is cool and soothing and it's the best time to induce up and opt for walk and exercise that rejuvenates the body and keep it active the whole day. Morning walk is healthier than evening walk because the exercise within the morning offer us probability to regain out mental and physical strength.

Another advantage of rising early within the term of health is "healthy breakfast". For a healthy man breakfast plays a very important role. It keeps a person energetic throughout the day. Those who rise early in the morning get their goals simply and higher than late riser as a result of former has longer to suppose or to consider their plans.

Prachi Gupta

Prachi Gupta is a student of BBA, hai ling from Allahabad, UP. She is fond of watching movies, travelling and cooking. Although, she loves writing and singing. As, she believes scribbling your thoughts on a blank paper can remove all your stress and makes a person happy. Along with this, she is a Digital Marketer and a Writer, who has been a co-author of many anthologies.

Follow her on instagram:- @_prachi_gupta_210

Not to Do

Not to Do
it is left and right
From six to nine
From A to B
I'm continuously turning around
Clock move and round
Mummy sounds so loud from the down
Papa standing upon my mouth.
It's too late and I am on my sleeping kip
Everyone is calling me out for a day.
Yet, still laying down on my bed
As, my couch combats me
"Not to Do It"

Ayesha Rajpal

Ayesha Rajpal is writer by passion. She is into nobel profession of teaching and runs an academy in Delhi. She is fun lovung and easy going person and has been co author for few books . She is into writing poems . Even she loves calligraphy and Mandala art too.

(1)

Lazy mornings Morning vibes are the best But we always wake up after birds leave their nest Waking up in the morning is what people like But lazy people like us sleeps day and night Night we enjoy and morning we sleep This is what youngsters nowdays like Roam around in the world Party all night is their trend But that's not right But yes morning wale ups are always the best But we always wake up after birds leave their nest

Shobha Rajpal

Shobha Rajpal is writer by passion. Her love for hindi is divine. She feels quite comfortable with hindi rather english as she loves her mother tongue. She is Hindi graduated and teacher by profession.

अँगड़ाई

फिर से वही सुबह और शाम है आई फिर से वहीं काली काली बदली है छाई कलियाँ दुल्हन की तरह शरमाई और मुझे तुम्हारी याद है आई वो बड़ी बड़ी आंखो की गहराई क्या बात थी जो समझ न आई वो मुझे देख कर बार बार मुस्काई तितलियों के छूने से फूलों पे बहार हैं छाई *वो अलसाई सी सुबह जब तुमने ली थींअँगड़ाई* आज मुझे बहुत याद है आई बहुत याद है आई

Shajeela Shamreen

Shajeela shamreen is a co author of many anthologies.she is currently pursuing a undergraduate degree in literature.she is on the process of becoming a well defined writer and soon she will achieve it. A strong dreamer basically,who wants to make those dreams true soon.

Madan's Entity

There lived a little boy Madan in a small family. He studies in school in a primary level.As every children denies to wake up early in the morning,Madan also does the same. His parents struggle a lot to wake him up in the morning and get him ready for school. Madan doesn't realise the importance of waking up early in the morning. He doesn't know that waking up in the morning can be so much beneficial to one. A successful entrepreneur or Businessman is made successful only through by waking up early in the morning. Normal person will not understand the ultimate benefits of waking up but the successful ones will realise it because they are successful due to this. If one wishes to achieve his/her dreams in their life they have to follow this.As Madan is a small boy he doesn't understand this initially. Madan mother will run behind him every morning to wake up him and to make him ready for school or to send him to other classes.His father used to scold him and warns him for doing like this regularly but Madan doesn't understand this or wanted to understand this. As Madan days was going on lazily and refusing to get up in morning, one day as he was sleeping his mother comes to wake him up and climb the stairs, suddenly she gets heart attack. She tries to call out Madan for help but as he is deep in sleep he doesn't hear his mother's voice.That time even madan's father was not there in home only he and his mother was left alone in home. His mother yells out,cries out in pain but Madan doesn't wake up at all. And at Last a tragedy happens in madan's life that is,his mother dies.He wakes up and comes down after two hours he sees his mother was lying down in staircase he tries to wake his mother up but she has no move at all in her body.he phones to his father and his father rushes to the home.His father calls doctor and doctor arrives and gives the news that madan's mother is no more. Madan gets great shock at that time and takes so many months to recover from that as in his young age only,then his father supports him and advises him that because of his laziness and refusion to wake up in the morning he lost his mother.That time only Madan realises his mistake and never repeated that mistake in his lifetime again. So one can understand from madan's life that resisting to wake up in the morning is bad at times too. we should not continuously refuse to wake up in the morning and we should get practice

Smriti Kumari

Smriti kumari is student by profession,writer by passion.she lives in Delhi,India. She is 2nd year student, pursuing bsc(h) maths from Rajdhani college,Delhi University. She is very passionate, inquisitive and hardworking for her work.she is also part of many anthologies.The pen is a strong weapon for her to portray her feelings.let's enjoy her writing and shower your love and support.

अंगड़ाइयां कुछ कहने लगी!

आंखें अभी आंख - मिचौली कर रही,
तभी सूरज भाई साहब ने
मेरे खिड़की से चुपके से दस्तक दे दी।
अब नींद को कौन समझाएगा ?
ये निकम्मी टूटने का नाम नहीं ले रही।
अब मम्मा भी लगी चिल्लाने -
"उठ जा कुंभकरण, कॉलेज का टाइम हो गया"।
धीरे धीरे मैं नींद को समझा रही ,
और पास के मोबाइल में टाइम देख रही!
सोच रही -" पांच मिनट और सो लेती हूं?
फिर उठकर जल्दी से रेडी हो लूंगी।
अब इन सारी उलझन में अंगड़ाई
कुछ कहने लगी!
मुझे आलस से झिंझोरने लगी।
अब थोड़ी देर में जाऊंगी नीचे!
यही सोचकर मैं दो मिनट सो गई!
अलार्म बजे, स्कूल की घंटियां भी बजी!
कॉलेज की लेक्चर भी शुरू हो गई!
पर मैं सोते रह गई।
और अंगड़ाइयां लोरी गाती रही।
मुझे सपनों में डुबाते रही!

Sahina Ghugha

Sahina Ghugha is 20 year old b.com student at Saurashtra university Rajkot. She is from Jamnagar city of Gujarat. She is state level winner in poetry competition 2017. She is Co-author of 10+ anthologies. She is an amazing writer and poet and she wants do something for society through her pen.

नया दिन नई चुनौती

आंखे खुली सूरज की किरणों से,
अंधेरे का परदा आंखो से हट गया।
एक नए दिन के लिए तेरा सुक्रीया खुदा,
एक और दिन जिंदगी से घट गया।

मन नहीं करता उठकर भाग चलने का,
जिंदगी की ये दौड़ कभी ख़तम ही नहीं होती।
पर भागना भी जरूरी है इस दौड़ में,
पीछे रहे जाने पर ये आंखे रो देती है।

उठ भी जाती बिस्तर से में कुछ ऐसे,
नये सपने, नई आशाएं हूं बुनती।
अंगड़ाई लेकर, रजाई हटा कर,
तैयार हूं मैं लेने एक नई चुनौती

Siya Golani

Siya golani is a creative writer. She has inclination to positive aspects of life. She is a confident presenter who keeps her views very subtle but firmly. She evokes her messages and effectively engages the audience through her writeups.

Good Morning

Chirping birds and satisfying rays is the morning's grace.
Such a pleasant weather and the happiness which is scattered.

Ringing alarms and chicken shouting in farms.
Makes me feel sleepier and then hitting snooze button in my alarm so that morning does not make me feel creepier.

But the fact is that
I have to get up and dress up.
Because I do not have to end being messed up.
But I feel sad because I do not want to leave my cozy bed.

Khushbu Rathore

An independent soul who likes to read, write, pants and design. A girl who, through poetry, expresses her feelings and enjoys comfort.

B. Ed is very talented girl with getting education. A proud girl from Pali district of Rajasthan receives her education during the day and most of her time in the night gives her time to the writing work. She is Khusbu Rathore and is delighted to be a part of this anthology

Instagram =@khushburathore1913

सुबह की अंगडाई

अंगडाई पर अंगडाई लेती है रात जुदाई की
इंतजार की आँधी से पूछ लो सबूत मेरी वफाई की
तुम क्या जानोंगे तुम क्या समझोगे सनम
तन्हाई भी रो पड़ी है सुनकर बात मेरी तन्हाई की
जब भी बरसात की रातों में बदन टूटता है
जाग उठती है अजब ख्वाहिशें अंगडाई की
वक़्त पर तो ये मौसम भी लेते है अंगडाई
फिर क्यू ज़माने से यहा सिर्फ में हू और मेरी तन्हाई
कुछ इस तरह प्यार जताती हू में
रात को उसको सपनों में देख
सुबह अंगडाई में भर लेती हू में
तुम फिर उसी अदा से अंगडाई लेके हंस दो
आ जाएगा पलट कर गुजरा हुआ ज़माना
सवांरकर जुल्फे जब को मेने अंगडाई
बहुत दिनों बाद दिल के आँगन में धूप आई है

अंगडाई के शब्द

देख के मुझे भरी महफिल में
चुपके के लेते है अंगडाई
कुछ शायरों की लफ्जों की
आपस में हुई खूब लड़ाई
"अ" ने कहा में पहला अक्षर
मुझसे ही हो आगाज
"ई" ने कहा बिना इश्क के
कौन शिरी कौन फरहाद
"ब" ने कहा बड़े तंगदिल हो
बात ना हो तो क्या बात हो
"व" ने कहा वक़्त पहलवान
सब कुछ खत्म ग़र वक़्त ना हो
देखकर उनकी आपसी रंजिश
"ख" से खुदा से रहा ना गया
बोले यह घमासान बंद हो
बिना बन्दगी इश्क पूरा न हुआ

Muskan Sachdeva

Muskan Sachdeva hails from Basti, uttar Pradesh. She completed studies from St. Basil's and is pursuing Chartered accountant along with bcom from Allahabad university. Writing was just a time pass earlier but then it became her passion. She has been co-authored in 10+ anthologies.

Morning's Sleep

The clock ticks 8 in morning
And soon mom starts saying "Get up it's 8"
Saying 5 more mins 5 more mins
We pass about 30 mins
The sleep at that time is so deep
It makes me dream of so beautiful things
Which I don't want to break
But who can win from a mother
Soon she will start shouting
"Get up it's too late"
And then I have break the dreams and get up
But the morning sleep at the time of getting up is often so sweet.

Lokesh Upadhyay

Lokesh Upadhyay, resident of buxar district in Bihar, presently he is a student in class 12th Dandi Swami sahajanand saint Vinova college. He has a keen interest in writing his heart out in the form of small poems, porses and verses. He hope you will enjoy reading his work and appreciate it.

Thank you..

वो पल , वो यादें।

सुबह उठते ही मुझे सबसे पहले तेरा ख्याल आता था,
अंगड़ाई लेने से भी पहले तेरा फोन आजाता था,
सूरज की रोशनी से पहले तेरा चेहरा देख के मेरा दिन सुरु होता था,
मुझ से पहले मेरा अंदर तू मुस्कुराता था,
सुबह सुबह तुझे देख के दिल सुकून से भर जाता था,
तेरी प्यारी सी अंगड़ाई और मुस्कान दिन बना देता था,
दिन की शुरुआत तेरी मुस्कान से और रात तेरी बात से होती थी,
तू हर पल मेरे साथ होता था,
पर अब वह सुबह की शुरुआत नहीं होती,
क्योंकि वह बात नहीं होती,
मेरे चेहरे पे वह मुस्कान नहीं होती,
सुबह की अंगड़ाई अब खास नहीं होती,
तू आश पास हो कर भी अब पास नहीं होता ,
आज वह प्यार की बरसात नहीं होता ,
क्योंकि अब एक अर्शा हुआ हमारी मुलाकात नहीं होता,
ओ पहले जैसी प्यार भारी बात नहीं होता,
तेरा मुझ से मिलने की अब वो फ़रियाद नहीं होता,
दिन तो गुजर जाता है ,
मगर ओ पहले वाली बात नहीं होता,
शायद तुम्हे अब किसी और से प्यार होने लगा है,
शायद तुम मुझे अब अपने दिन से निकालने लगे हो,
शायद अब तुम्हारा मन भर गया है इस रिश्ता से,
शायद अब तुम्हे नए लोगो की जरूरत है,
शायद अब मै तुम्हे अच्छा न लगता,
शायद अब मुझे भी छोड़ देना चाहिए तुम्हारा पीछा ,
लेकीन यार क्या इतना आसान होता है अपने प्यार को भुलाना,
बस एक बार आओ,

आके मुझे अपने दिल की बात बताओ,
यदि तुम्हे सही में मेरे से दूर जाके खुशी मिलती है ,
तब तो तुम आराम से जाओ ,
मै भी छोड़ दूंगा तुम्हारा पीछा,
लेकीन कभी भी मेरा जरूरत पड़े तो बस एक बार याद करना ,
जितना प्यार कल था ,
इतना ही आज है,
और खुद पे बिस्वास है कि कल भी रहेगा।
तुम्हारा लोकेश कल भी तुम्हारा था , और रहेगा।
बहुत सारा प्यार।

Ujjwal Shree

Ujjwal shree with her pen name Neha Gupta is from Patna, Bihar

She is an avid writer, poetess, and artist. She loves to play with words and write from the depth of her heart. She always express her emotions through words rather than saying. She generally writes about Motivation, emotions, pain and abstract. Writing helps her to survive in her worst phase of life. Writing is just like breathing to her because when she feels depressed she used to write her feelings.

Follow her on Instagram : @Shree22349

Email Id : ng223494@gmail.com

Person Who Gets Up Early...Rise Early

I used to be a regular lazy girl who had the habit of waking up at 12 in the afternoon. This was one of the major reasons why I used to get scolded by my family members on a regular basis.

I tried many a time to get rid of this bad practice but all in vain. Maybe I never had a solid reason to do so.

But now things has changed when I joined my college. Now I wake up to my alarm no matter what now and basically hop out of bed on auto pilot.

Personally, I set 3 alarms. If I want to get up at 6, I set a 6 AM alarm, one at 6:05, and my last alarm on a different clock across the room at 6:10. The first 2 alarms let me start to wake up, sort of like a warm start, and usually prevents the "dead weight" and foggy feeling.

I make breakfast, brush my teeth, or plop into a chair and look at memes for 20 minutes while I wake up. It doesn't matter as long as that last alarm is absolute.

Eventually, I adjusted to this and it wakes me no matter what time I need to get up. I just hop out of bed automatically when I hear that third alarm.

This is all I follow and it works for me like a charm.

Thanks for all the attention!!

Prakash Sharma

"लिख देते है हम दिल के अल्फ़ाज़ युही सुबह - शाम
लफ्ज़ है जो गहरे इतने की ये है बस तेरी मोहब्बत के नाम"

Prakash Sharma is a writer, poet, shayar and author. He writes poem, shayari and quotes which are attach with the life, reality, love and motivation. In personal life he is a student of Law and Chartered Accountancy. You can find him at www.penofshayar.blogspot.com.

तेरी यादें

रातों में जो रोज नींद नही आती मुझको,
और सुबह को देर तक जो सोने लगा हूं,
कभी मेरी तो कभी तेरी,
यादों में अब खोने लगा हूं।

यूं तो आजकल वक़्त भी बेजुबान हो गया है,
जब हमने खुदसे ही उम्मीद छोड़ दी है,
मुदत्त तक चाहने पर भी उनका न मिलना,
तब खुद की तक़दीरें मोड़ ही दी है।

बेवक़्त इस जुबान पर नाम जो आ जाता है,
सुबह - शाम उनका,
खुद मे कभी हँसने तो कभी रोने लगा हूं,
कभी मेरी तो कभी तेरी,
यादों में अब खोने लगा हूं,
रातों में जो रोज नींद नही आती मुझको,
और सुबह को देर तक जो सोने लगा हूं।

अंगड़ाइयां

रोज - रोज उन कोरे पन्नो पर कुछ लिखने की दास्तान,
चाय की महक कर देती है कुछ बातें बेज़ुबान।

कभी कभी सारी बातों का हम इज़हार नही कर सकते,
रोज लडकर रोज झगडकर भी तुझसे प्यार नही कर सकते।

हालात भी मजबूर है मेरे तुम पूछो तो सही,
बोहोत से दर्द इस दिल ने छुपा रखे है अभी।

रात से सुबह हो या फिर हो अकेली शाम,
बातों ही बातों में आता है तेरा नाम।

सोच समझकर कर देते है इन लफ़्ज़ों को बयां,
कभी हँसकर कभी रोकर बताती जिंदगी मेरी जान।

चाय की चुस्की हो या हो बातों की गहराइयाँ,
कुछ अच्छा लिखने पर ले लेता हूं अंगड़ाइयां।

पसंद आई कविता तो शुक्रियां आपका जनाब,
मौज मस्ती में जीते रहिये अब अलविदा और आदाब।

Ashwini Kumar Singh

He is Ashwini, a budding pharmacist from Delhi. He has been writing quotes and poems since long back but never thought of writing them for publication purpose . It is because of his friend that he has entered in this field . He is very thankful to that friend of his .

That Beautiful Morning ...

Beautiful mornings are those ,
When you get up and yawn ,
and the rising sun looks like rose .

Lost in that Divinity ,
unaware of happenings in visinity ,
I was looking up high ,
towards gleaming sky .

Sun was rising ,
World seemed cherishing ,
I was praying ,
May this morning ,
Be everlasting ...

Neha. M

Meet this young Indian writer who prescients the minor aspects of life to the world through her admirable perspective. She who is striving to create her world of literature artistically. You can find more of her work on insta as deepin_ink.

The Mornings Of Choices

How do I explain the world that not everyone wakes up by the roaring of a clock?

Some wrestling the responsibilities and some buried in a pool of worries.

The morning sun conjuring its beauty of black, blue and white;

A slaying transition as the fleet of birds takes their flight.

How do I explain the world that the mornings are always a choice to rise brave or remain as it is?

Some articulate it as a new beginning and some believe it's still the same thing.

While the day light takes its course of every shade and a ray of benevolence;

A sun rise and it's reflections for some people still remains a choice.

सवेरा

अंधेरे से लिपते रात को जब सवेरा मोडता है,
हम पंछियों के आवाज से समय नाप लेते है|
कुछ बात होती होगी अंधेरे उझाले के बीच शायद,
हमारे सुकून को छीन फिर हमें उलझा जाने की|

Saurabh Rajput

लेखक को "सौरभ राजपूत" के नाम से जाना जाता है
और हमें शायरी ,कविताएं , और गानों का सौंख है
और हां कोई दुःखी हो तो उसे हंसाने का भी....!

अंगड़ाई....

वह जो आई तुम्हारी यादों
दिल ने ली अंगड़ाई है।
भीगे तेरी नजाकत से हम
लगा इश्क की बरसात आई है।
कहीं रंग हुए बेजान मिल
तेरे इश्क का रंग फितूर चढ़ा
जैसे इश्क का रंगरेज कोई
मेरी रूह को भी रंग रहा...
मैं जिस्म भले पर तू मेरी
लगती प्यारी परछाई है
वह जो आई तुम्हारी याद
दिल ने ली अंगड़ाई है।.

Vedika Agarwal

She is Vedika Agarwal a student of Bsc home science, Delhi university. She likes to write and draw a sketch. She is passionate for dancing, singing and acting. She is a determined, bold and a kind hearted girl. She is very conducive in nature. She loves to spend her leisure with old age home people and orphanage children. She loves to learn new things. She is a very emotional girl. She loves to write. She has a very helpful and loving nature towards the people. She is very meek and humble. She wants to explore the innovative things in the very positive manner. If anyone stabs her at the back she totally gets shattered. She is a very trustworthy and a reliable girl.

Ek Shuruat Subha Ke Saath

Voh subha subha uthke
Surya uda dekhna
Uski roshni se sari jagah ka roshan hona
Aur hmare chehre pe roshni padna
Aisa lagta hai mano Zindagi se andhera ja raha ho
Aur Chidiyon ki char prahat sunna
Dil ko ek rahat sa deta hai

Voh subha subha
Shaanti main ghumna
Hawa ka Muh ko chuke nikalna
Ek ehsaas sa chhod jata tha

Voh pedo ke beech se
Prayavran se saans lena
Aur voh subha subha ki Chai
Ek tazagi si chhod jati thee

Voh subha subha uthna
Aur yoga karna
Apne shareer Ko swasth banana
Pure dinn ki thakavat mita deta tha

Der se soke uthna
Ek Aalas sa chhod jata h pura dinn ke liye
Par subha jldi uthke vyayam krna
Aalas nai aane Deta pure dinn

Rat rat bhar kam karna
jiski vjh se subha late uthte hai
Jo ki galat hai

Kaam ke saath saath apna Dhyan rkhna bahut zaroori hai

Par aaj Kal ke log
Kaam main itna mashroof hogye hai
Ki unko apne shareer se zyda Kaam se Pyar hai
Logo ko apne jeevan main cheezo Ko ek hi tarazoo main rakhke barabar tolna Chahiye

Subha subha uthke padne se
Har Kaam aasan ho jata hai
Dimag acha hota hai
Aur cheeze yaad Aasani se Ho jati hai
Shaanti main Sara Dhyan ekagrit karke
Jisse Aapke Kaam ko pura hone main safal bnata hai

Har ek kamyab Insaan ka peeche ka raz hai
Subha uthke apne Kaam pe Dhyan dena
Mehnat karna Aur apne shareer ka Dhyan rkhna
Yeh hoti hai ek safal insaan Ki Zindagi

Shubham Kumar

Shubham Kumar is 19 years old From Bihar. He is the Student of Engineering.

He had started writing since 2018.

He Writes pretty Good, And Mostly About Love and Sad.

He have the Skills, Idea and Creativity For the Writing.

He is Co-author in 6 Anthology.

He is always blessed that everyone appreciate him.

सुबह की अंगराई हो संग तुम्हारे

सुबह की अंगराई हो संग तुम्हारे
एक हसीन रात के बाद
थोड़ी सी मुस्कान और थोड़ी सी शर्म्र हो
आंखों में तुम्हारे ।

एक छोटी सी ख्वाहिश है मेरी
तुम हर सुबह, मेरे बाहों में लो अंगराई
सुबह की सफर शुरू हो एक कप चाय से
और खत्म तुम्हारी बांहों में लिपटने से ।

तुम्हारी जुल्फें, तुम्हारी होंठों को परेशान करे
तो मैं अपने उंगलियों से उन्हें तुम्हारे होंठों से जुदा कर
उन होंठों को अपना बनाऊं ।

फिर तुम आईने के सामने खुद की खुबसूरती की तारीफ करते
करते
हल्की सी तुम अंगराई लो
और मैं पीछे से आकर तुम्हें अपने बाहों में ले लूं
तुम चाहो जितना बचना, मैं तुम्हारे होंठों को फिर से अपना बना लूं ।

छोटी सी ख्वाहिश है, ऐसी एक सुबह हो
जितनी दफा लो तुम अंगराई
मैं तुम्हें पीछे से अपने बाहों में लेकर
तुम्हें अपना बना लूं ।।

Abhishek Rawat

Born and brought up in Prayagraj, the city of Kumbh. Born on December 3rd. A tax advisor by profession but a writer at heart. A believer in the saying that feelings are best expressed with words.

My Lazy Morning

I woke up one morning,
To find everyone else asleep.
I switched the TV on, yawning,
And opened the window for a peep.

The town awoke in slow motion,
Trying to search it's way.
As if it had, had a drowsy potion,
The effect of which was frizzling away.

On my way to open the door,
I found a river of spilt milk on the floor.
A cat would have looked up to see what's in store.
A good look at me, she thought of asking for more.

Soon the golden rays of sunshine shone,
Expressing eloquently like it was time.
The birds were flying to unknown grounds,
Amidst the silence, there were waves of sound.

I went by the bedside and pulled the sheet,
It was a lazy morning, so I deserved a treat.
I lay asleep for a little more while,
The world looked happy and I looked fine.

Debanjana Ghatak

Debanjana is a simple girl and down to earth by nature. By profession she is an English Faculty at a reputed Educational Institution. She is an ardent lover of Nature, animals, Literature and a believer of God. She loves to dream and enjoy dwelling in her fairy tale land. She loves to enjoy the tiny rays of happiness hidden in the smallest moments of life. In short she describes herself as a dreamer and believer. Whenever she felt the presence and beauty of love and got smell of Nature, a new poetry or a story took birth. She believes in the philosophy of never giving up. She doesn't give up dreaming and believing in what she believes.

Wake Up, It's 9 Am Already

Birds are chirping outside and the clock says it's 4:30 am. Rose is busy watching her favorite Netflix series. 'It's 4:30 am already but my series is still left. Alright I will watch it in the midnight. Time to bed.' Rose said to herself and went to sleep.

'Rose, wake up, how long will you sleep? It's already 7:30.' Rose's mom called her but she is in deep slumber.

After sometime, 'Rose, Rose, can you hear me? It's already 9 am and you are still sleeping? Don't you feel ashamed of yourself?

'Mom, it's just 9 am I'll wake up after 15 mins.'

'Rose, it's 9:30 and if you don't wake up now then see what I'll do to you.'

Rose wakes up and after sometime goes back to sleep again. Her mom entered her room once again and saw her sleeping.

'Rose, you didn't wake up? Breakfast is ready. I am fed up of you. From tomorrow you'll prepare your own breakfast. You are just too much to handle.

Rose finally wakes up from her sleep at 9:45 am and said, 'mom, I went to sleep at 4:30 am so I must sleep till 11 am at least but you wake me up. I'm feeling so much sleepy. Rose's mom looks at her angrily and goes back to kitchen.

Pratham Mittal

Pratham Mittal
He is very Positive, kind, helpful, friendly and happy soul. His passion is painting and writing. He has won many competitions, published in many books, participated in international writing competitions.

(1)

Wake up In the Morning.
After you said your prayer.
Or didn't.
Least wakeup in the morning with a smile.

After you thank him.
Or you didn't.
Wake up in the morning with a smile.

With each heartbeat.
Be thankful.
With each walk.
Be grateful.
You wake up in the morning with a smile.

Things we should be so thankful for.
Always centers around the blessing of the lord.

Pragya Verma

Pragya Verma is from Prayagraj, Uttar Pradesh. She is currently pursuing Bachelor's in Computer Application from Ewing Christian College, Prayagraj. She is a poet and a writer. She has done many anthologies as a co-author and currently compiling her own anthology. She has a great interest in making paintings and doing photography. You can follow her on Instagram: @wordsofpragya

School Life

Those times of our childhood,
When we don't want to go to school.
We resist to wake up in the morning,
Until our mother gave us last warning.
And then we wake up with a yawn.

We used to hate that school starts at dawn.
Yawning while our maths class was going on.
We just used to watch until our teacher gone.
Everyone just eagerly waits for the break,
To share food and beat friends until it ache.

Those fights, share and care,
I couldn't find anywhere.
Colleges don't have those sparks,
It has memories of my darks.
I always miss my childhood days,
It's memories come up like smokey haze.

School friends don't leave you alone,
They can make you smile by becoming a clown.
School friends stay together forever,
They don't cheat and don't play like a clever.
School days are best days of life,
It has the beautiful memories of our life.

Siya Golani

Siya Golani is a creative writer. She has inclination to positive aspects of life. She is a confident presenter who keeps her views very subtle but firmly. She evokes her messages and effectively engages the audience through her writeups.

Good Morning

Chirping birds and shining rays is the morning's grace,
Such a pleasant weather and the happiness which is scattered.

Ringing alarm and chicken shouting in farms, make me feel sleepier and then hitting the snooze button in my alarm so that the morning does not make me feel creepy.

but the fact is that I have to get up and dress up because I do not have to end being messed up.
But I feel sad because I do not want to leave my cosy bed.

Jainab Natchiya. Y

Jainab Natchiya. Y is a beginner and completed her Master Degree in Business Management. Currently, She is tutor and have a passion in photography and writing.

Resistance Of Getting Up In The Morning

Feeling the smoothness of mattress below my body;
Cuddling with my romantic fluffy pillow;
Wrapped by the warmness of blanket;
Still craving for more Night to pass.

Battling myself to come out from my Dreamland;
Somehow I open my eyes by the glance of sunlight hitting my skin;
The brightness reminds of my Goal and push me to Rise and shine.
Eventually, I arouse leaving my love behind
and we knew that at the end of the day,
we gonna be together again by
hitting the sack.

Sanoj Kumar

He is an engineer, started writing two years back never imagined that people would like it, and feel his emotions as theirs. He also likes to express other's feelings and always try to change other's mindsets in a better way through his writings. Nowadays he is a member of many writing communities and earned lots of certificates through his writings. His first book as an author is launched from a " poetry world organization " named as " सफ़र, जिन्दगी का ". " Fam-Bond in lockdown " is his first anthology as a compiler and editor while he is a co-author of many anthologies.

You can see his poetry on Instagram @the_hidden_writer_sk
And an article on blogger
@http://safarzindagikask.blogspot.com
Contact him through his mail id
@thehiddenwritersk@gmail.com

अंगड़ाई

सब कहते है उठो सवेरे,
मुझसे तो ये होता नहीं।
काम हो या ना हो फिर भी,
2 बजे से पहले सोता नहीं।

पता है मुझे उठना चाहिए जल्दी,
क्या करूं उठ कर फिर सो जाता हूं।
मां चिल्ला चिल्ला कर थक जाती,
पर मैं अंगड़ाई लेकर सोते रहता हूं।

जड़ा सोचो, हमारा क्या कसूर है,
अच्छी नींद भी तो सुबह ही आती है।
हल्की ठंड के साथ ये गर्म मौसम,
इसलिए सुबह की नींद सबको भाती है।

Kalamkaar

This is kalamkaar. He is from uttrakhand but broughtup in meerut. His hobbies are reading and writing. He love writing. He is part of 200+Anthology as co- author and won 150+certificate in writing. He is simple and people observer.

अंगड़ाई

सपनो की दुनिया में हम खोये होते हैं !
जब हम सुबह सोये होते हैं !
सूरज निकल गया जल्दी जैसे ऐसा लगता हैं !
उठने में कस्ट थोड़ा होता हैं !
बिस्तर छोड़कर बाहर निकलने का मन नहीं होता हैं !
माँ होती गुस्सा बोलती उठजा जल्दी कितना तू सोता हैं !
कम तुझसे कुछ नहीं होता हैं !
मैं आलास में लेटा रहता बिस्तर पकड़कर, मुश्किल होता बिस्तर छोड़ना !
हटाके चद्दर मैं हिम्मत जुटाता !
खुदको में बड़ी मुश्किल से बिस्तर से अलग कर पता !
2 मिनट का टाइम मांगके मम्मी से फिर से सो जाता !
मन को मैं मनाता फिर से उठने कि कोशिश में लग जाता !
पड़ना जाये मार मम्मी से हिम्मत हार के में बिस्तर से उठ जाता !
हाथ मुँह धोकर दिन मर्रा के कामो में लग जाता !

Shivam Sinha

Shivam Sinha is a poet, a writer, book reviewer, blogger, and co-author of 3 anthologies. He has been writing for 2+ years and is a rhymester . He has an optimistic approach towards life. According to him, writing is the only way to express your feelings. He loves to write from personal experiences and words help him portray his feelings.

His contribution includes

poetry, quotes, short stories mostly related to romance, relationship, and friendship. He believes that "Beyond the stars, our fate lies". You can contact him at instantpoetry.love@gmail.com or you can ping him on his Instagram ID.

(1)

वो सुबह की नींद और प्यारी अंगड़ाई...
सुबह उठने की ये प्रथा किसने बनाई??
कितना भी चाहूं, मुझसे उठा नहीं जाता,
पर ये बात मैं किस किस को समझाता...

लोग कैसे उठ जाते हैं इतनी जल्दी??
मुझे कोई तो बताए...
मेरी नींद और अंगड़ाई... हाए!!

वो हर सुबह मां का मुझे उठाना...
और मेरा फिर से सो जाना...

वो सुबह की नींद और प्यारी अंगड़ाई...
नींद पूरी करने को करनी पड़ती है लड़ाई...
ये आलास मुझसे छोड़ा ना जाए,
सुबह की नींद और अंगड़ाई...हाए!!

Yamini Sona Vaishnavi

Yamini sona Vaishnavi is a budding writer who is pursuing her III UG of English Literature . She started writing from her school days by contributing to magazines and she continued the same in her college too . She is already a co-author for 6 anthologies . She loves writing and playing with words and has wishes to reach the hearts of readers through her poetry so that her thoughts will reach them in a more better way .

The Battle at Dawn !

I've heard people telling and uttering dictions ...
Including so many stuffs of routine variance ...
I wonder their capacity ...
And marvel at their abilities ...
How do they win the everyday battle ?

I say it a battle because , I feel more anxious ...
My bliss of getting extra nap is disturbed so tremendous ...
The alarm I set , screams so intolerable ...
But the way I look at it is so disgraceful...
How do they win the everyday battle ?

I see many of my close and well known confidants...
The living and Victorious examples who are evident ...
I set my biological clock even when it pours hail...
To start with a walk which as usual fail ...
How do they win the everyday battle ?

My final try of winning the everyday battle ...
I feel determined to avoid living a life of a driven cattle ...
I go to bed as early as possible and set my mind ....
With god's boon I wake up early and that's how the way I find...
How did I the win the battle which I fought all along ?
The battle between me and dawn !

Sunil Kimidi

Sunil Kimidi named person was gifted to this world by Ramu & Mani on 1995/12/24. He worked as CAD engineer in Visakhapatnam. His contents are full of patriotism and respect for women. The essence in his writings attracts everyone. Just as there are many stars unseen in the sky, so many beautiful feelings that we do not see are hidden in his heart.

"Fresh Minds"

You will have a lot of strength when you wake up early in the morning. Your brain will help you to take perfect decisions. You can think about everything as long as you want. Nothing will obstruct you from good mood. You can get a fresh mind everyday if you wake up early. The cold breeze in the morning gives you relief from you tensions. The environment provides you a chance for studying and doing something interesting you need. As our elders said, those who read in the morning will make the perfect outputs. They will have the fresh minds. So, we can easily absorb anything according to our wish. We can get more energy physically and mentally.

Pragyan Panda

Pragyan is persuing her B.Tech in "Chemical Engineering" from IGIT, Sarang. She's a short girl from Rourkela, Odisha. With fascination of nature, she's a spiritual person who motivates people. She does weird stuff like interacting with non living ones and pens down her mind. For more of her works, do follow her IG @quote_love_97.

Bliss of Rest

The sun rises but it's my midnight;
They keep shouting;
But its my habit.

Call it hostel disease_
But seriously restless nights;
Maybe morning peace.

Got ample to do even after trying:
Believe me! no sunrise views;
Even after million crying.

Either current or mumma disturbs_
The bliss of rest;
With enough comments and stupid proverbs.

Though I try to change and study,
But my bed and pillows_
Damn make me moody.

Hell night shifts are pleasure;
Until mornings are wasted
But for me, there's no escape of this gesture.

Hema Kirthiga J

She is Hema Kirthiga J, and her pen name is sparkle. She is professionally a psychologist and passionately a writer. She heals others but writing heals her. She is writer, reader, orator and a believer. She is from Chennai. She lives by the principal of inspire and be inspired. She writes her heart and soul and she deeply believes that the depth of her heart and the nib of her pen are soulfully connected. Writing is an art and she is a proud artist. She loves what she does and loves what she writes. You can reach her at

Instagram- @the_pen_queen
Email- inker.sparkle@gmail.com
Yourquote – JKM

Few Minutes Of Heaven

I Didn't sleep well last night!
With all the over thinking!
With all the reality hitting on my face!
With all the pain!
But I don't know why now!!
I never want to get up!!
The bed was like rock last night!
But now its the most softest!
I couldn't sleep in the night silence!
But now my alarm sounds like a lullaby!
Maybe I am not ready to face life!
I just want to stay in the few minutes of heaven.

Vikash Kumar Bhakat

Vikash Kumar Bhakat is a poet, author, novelist, writer, teacher and a social & educational entrepreneur from Shankarda village near Jamshedpur,Jharkhand. The poet is also the President of Vikash Educational & Charitable Trust. He has completed his graduation in English Language & Literature securing first class position. He imparts free English education to the underprivileged students in Janamdih a tribal dominated village under Potka Block of East Singhbhum, Jharkhand

Yawning in Morning

I woke up yawning
Early in the morning
Birds were chirping
Wind was blowing
Dragonflies were flying
Sun was rising
I was yawning
I was thinking
What was happening
I found nothing
Only I was smiling
It was amazing
I was really enjoying

(2)

A yawning morning
I saw a mouse was nibbling something
I was busy in my work
I slept late in night
It was my right
Work was tight
There was no light
I had to fight
With my sight
It was my lot
I tried a lot
I hit a shot
And It was caught
It was a pussycat
In my hut
And a mouse
Was nibbling a nut
It was yawning
I saw in the morning

Ekta Pankaj Bathija

एकता. पी .बठीजा का जन्म बैंगलोर में हुआ है। वो साइरा के नान से भी लिखती है।उन्होंने १० साल की उम्र से लिखना शुरू किया था।वक़्त के साथ - साथ उनके लिखने का तरीका तथा स्तर भी बदलता गया। उनके हिसाब से लिखना हमारे मन के भावनाओ को दर्शाता है ।

सपनो का दुश्मन

सूरज की मधुर किरणे
समुन्दर को चमका रही हैं
बहती लहरें किनारे छू रही हैं
मुक्त गगण में पंछी गा रहे हैं
दुनिया की खूबसूरती का मज़ा
हम भी उठा रहे हैं

हवाओं के झोकों मैं
मधुर स्वर सी आयी
मदहोश होकर हम
उस और खींच आये

हर रोज़ की तरह,
फिर वहीं बैठी दिखी तुम
हाथों में वही गिटार लिए
वही गाना बजाए

अलार्म की घंटी,
तुमसे दूर खींच ले जाए

क्या करे बेचारे हम
तुम्हे देख नही पाए

अध जगे सपने की डोर
हम खिंचते चले जाते
फिर उसी पल में हम ,दुबारा पोहोंच जाते

आज चेहरा देखने की बात
दिल ने ठानी
पर उस प्यार के दुश्मन ने
फिरसे घंटी बजाई

आखिर नींद टूट गयी
हमने ली अंगड़ाई
मन तो बहोत है ,सपनो में लौटने का
ताकी तुम तक पोहोंच पाए
मगर जाना है आफिस
कहीं देर ना हो जाये।।

Swayamdeepta Das

She is Swayamdeepta Das,residing in Hindmotor,a suburban town in Hooghly district of West Bengal.She has passed class 12 from Vivekananda Academy and will pursue engineering.She loves music,sketching and is an ardent reader of crime fiction.She is a co-author of 40+ anthologies.She is a realistic person.She has also compiled and edited a book 'Pure Bliss' which is going to be published soon.
Instagram-swayamdeepta_das

Waking Up

Getting up in the morning might turn out to be a Herculean task
Especially for a nocturnal creature like me
Our present generation stays glued to the mobile screen
Upto late at night which keeps us fast asleep in the morning
Also a feeling of laziness prevails
We don't feel like leaving the cosiness of our bed
Don't we love to wander in our world of dreams?
Far away from the problems of the real world
So we cling tightly to our side pillow
And keep requesting for five minutes more of sleep
That ultimately drags on to half an hour or even more!
But we fail to remember that we must get up
And struggle to fulfil our beautiful dreams
Only then our life will be worthwhile.

Shivani Taneja

Shivani Taneja, born and raised in Delhi, India. A freelancer writer working on publishing my own book, a blogger who loves to write more for herself. I'm a creator and editor of - _soulfulbeing_ I love to inspire people with my thoughts and experiences. I created this page to post my thoughts and you can see and taste some of my work. You can call it my public playground!

Resistance of Getting Up in The Morning

Not able to sleep at night just because of the thought of having dream's. Dream's can break you, make you, destroy you, make you feel restless and above all of them, can build you up. Resisting myself from waking up in the morning has become a routine. Those responsibilities and roles that have been imposed on me before a certain age have made me feel so restless that at times I resist myself from waking up.

But it feels like ki those responsibilities are more active than I am. Waking up before me, knocking my mind everytime I start to feel a bit low, making me realize my worth. This is all what responsibility does. Waking up has become a task these days that i have to perform on a daily basis. But I wish to have those carefree nights back where waking up was not a to do thing on daily basis, but was a must thing to do.

Those nights when I used to dream and there was no hurry of waking up and I do not have to resist myself basically from waking up, where the days when I used to live for myself. Fortunately, this is the time when I have to push myself up every other morning to wake up and make up myself for the day.

These days I prefer resisting myself from waking up and have those dreams relived again.

Chirag L Sagar

Chirag L Sagar is a 1st year MBBS student studying at Srinivas Institute of Medical Sciences and Research Centre,Mangalore. His hobbies are poetry, reading - books,novels, autobiographies,philately, listening to songs,sports like cricket and badminton,cooking. He is a medico by profession and a writer by passion. His best friend Nihar,has always been his inspiration and motivation to do great in whatever he does. His dream is to become an Oncologist and a successful writer.

Instagram : @chirag_cls18 Facebook
Chirag LSagar

(1)

Cold mornings with a shade of sunlight is something to which none can say no.

(2)

Gloomy mornings make sure that you won't have a bad day, as you'll be forced to stay on bed

Ajay Poddar 'Anmol

He is Ajay Poddar 'Anmol' from kolkata, mainly his most of works started from Uttrakhand he used to live in Madhyapradesh he is the only person in his family who loves literature because he thinks only literature and positive literacy can change the world and society after 7 years of struggle he entered in literature fully by professional development from dream analysis,He want to proof that universal fact literature is directly proportional to science and science is directly proportional to god and god is directly proportional to literature

अंगड़ाई

किसी कहानी का नया अवतार लिए,
सुबह होता है एक नई शुरुआत लिए,
कोई लेता है अंगड़ाई चाय पीने के किये,
कोई लेता है दो वक्त की रोटी कमाने के लिए,
बड़ी नायाब चीज है अंगड़ाई,
नए हौंसलो में जान भरने के लिए,
नन्ही सी चिड़िया के उड़ान भरने के लिये,
थैले में दफ्तर का सामान भरने के लिए,
बच्चे की किलकारी का गान भरने के लिए,
नई उम्मीदों का सफर फिर शुरू हो जाता है,
अंगड़ाई के साथ ताजा हर जुनून हो जाता है,
उमंगों की जमीन को एक नया आसमान मिलता है,
किसानों को खिला सा खलियान मिलता है,
खिलाड़ी को अपनी ओर बुलाता मैदान मिलता है,
अंगड़ाई के साथ सिर्फ आँखे नहीं खुलती,
खुलता है एक नई दिशा का पिटारा,
सुबह की अंगड़ाई बनती है सुकून का पिटारा,
अंगड़ाई चिकित्सक की नई दवा होती है,
पुजारी की जीती-जागती दुआ होती है,

पिता के कर्मो का बखान करती है,

विद्यार्थियों में नई सी जान भर्ती है,

अंगड़ाई खुदमें अद्‌भुत है,

अंगड़ाई नव जीवन का साक्ष्य है,

यह स्वयं ही सकारात्मक पक्ष है,

इसका निराला अपना नक्स है,

उन्नति ही तो इसका लक्ष्य है,

अंगड़ाई स्वप्नों को सजग बना देती है,

सत्य को यह अमर बना देती है,

जीत में बदलकर कल की हार को,

आज नई प्रहर सजा देती है,

अंगड़ाई जो ले पुष्प कभी,

तो यह पूरे जग को महका देती है,

कोयल की मधुर पुकारो से,

मुर्ग के जागरण मंत्रो से,

आधुनिक कई यंत्रो से,

खिल उठती है अंगड़ाई,

अंगड़ाई यलगार भी है,

समस्त सुखों का दरकार भी है,

डाकिए का इंतजार हुआ करता था,

कबूतर भी पैगाम दिया करता था,

विचित्र विचारक है अंगड़ाई,

वह प्रातः कुछ शीघ्र हुआ करता था,

मातृ शक्ति का श्रृंगार है अंगड़ाई,

पुरुषत्व जा प्रमाण है अंगड़ाई,

Dr Rakesh R Mund

Dr Rakesh R Mund has been participating in more than 70 anthology and his solo books are ishq-e-panhi & Vidhwansh available on amazon, flifpkart and others platform. He read veda and diffrent literatures which give a glimpse on his writing. You can contact with him : insta- Rakeshmundr_

अंगडाई

जख्म़ देकर जिंदगी लेती अंगडाई
मुझे देख अकसर बुलाती अंगडाई

रुहानी है तेरा मिलना मुझसे जाना
रूठ जाऐ तो हमेशा दिखाती अंगडाई

तसीर -ए- मोहब्बत उसको है पता
कभी हसीं देकर कभी रुलाती अंगडाई

अहल -ए- जाहाँ समझाकरो इशारा मेरा
ग़र नासमझ रहोगे तभी तडपाती अंगडाई

इल्तिफ़ात देखकर उसके झोकों में न आ
खूद का रस्ता चुनकर महकती अंगडाई

दोस्तों के संग रहकर अंजुमन-आरा किया
सरज़निश-ए-ख़ल्फ़ हमको मिलाती अंगडाई

यूं तु भी है उस मोहल्ले में सामिल "राकेश"
छोड़कर जाना नहीं कहाँ पकड़ती अंगडाई

Flairs and Glairs, a platform by a student for the students. We are esteemed youth struggling to carve out our path for our future and we follow a basic mindset Since everyone is not born with all-round skills. Joining hands with people who are born to execute it with perfection is the best way to evolve. Self-Evolution is the need of the hour but, evolving as a community is what we strive for. The initiative as kickstarted by, Founder- Mr. Shubham Shah with the motive to utilize the skillset and talent of writing has now a team of 10+ people who are actively participating into newer forms of learning and discovering talents among youngsters. We Provide platform and services like Publishing opportunities, Open mics, Workshops, Hands-on training. Operating with Brand Name Of Flairs and Glairs (Publication House), we offer the chance of elevating a passionate writer to an esteemed author With Brand name Teekhe Zasbaaat, We bring to you an opportunity to get accustomed with the Public Speaking and Presenting of Thoughts along with regular challenges to brush up your inking spirit. The newest initiative to extend our services we introduced in a new writing Platform- The Glittering Fables and Ink Over Tears.

We Choose to Fly Like A Falcon than to be a

Leg Pulling Crab.

To Know More: Infoline – 7781900870
Mail Us At-
flairsandglairs@gmail.com / info@flairsandglairs.in
Or Visit is at
www.flairsandglairs.com / www.flairsandglairs.in
Social Handles- @flairsandglairs @teekhezasbaaat

www.ingramcontent.com/pod-product-compliance
Ingram Content Group UK Ltd.
Pitfield, Milton Keynes, MK11 3LW, UK
UKHW022005190726
13853UKWH00004B/1736